YouTube

Colin Terrell
Michael Terrell

First published in Great Britain by Axis Education Ltd.

ISBN 978-1-84618-195-5

Axis Education, PO Box 459
Shrewsbury, SY4 4WZ

Email: enquiries@axiseducation.co.uk
www.axiseducation.co.uk

Grinning and laughing, Wayne stood up and shouted at Mr Martin, his history teacher.

'You trying to tell us that just 'cos this guy Hitler killed a load of Jews, you think he was bad? To me, that sounds like he was a really fuckin' cool dude.'

Jack, who was sitting next to Wayne, took out his mobile phone. He pressed the video start button. They'd planned this. The film was going up on YouTube.

The boys had been taking the piss out of Mr Martin for weeks. But this time it was going global.

Wayne stood up and turned around to face the class. Holding out his arms he shouted, 'Come on guys. Let's hear it for Hitler!'

The whole class stood up clapping, cheering and yelling. Giving each other high-fives.

Mr Martin stared at the class. Eyes wide open. Shocked.

This kind of thing had been going on for weeks. Always started by Wayne and Jack.

Finally, Mr Martin totally lost it. He grabbed a chair.

Wayne was still shouting and facing the class. He didn't see Mr Martin move up behind him.

The teacher brought the chair down hard on Wayne's head. Hitting the boy, Mr Martin yelled the same word over and over again.

'Bastard... Bastard... Bastard!'

Wayne went down with the first blow. As soon as Mr Martin had started hitting him the class had gone quiet. For a few seconds there was complete silence.

Wayne lay on the floor and Mr Martin just kept hitting him with the chair.

Then everybody in the classroom started shouting and screaming again. But this time they were afraid. A group of pupils were pushing and struggling to get out of the door.

Two teachers who had heard the first lot of yelling burst into the room.

They pulled Mr Martin away from Wayne.

Wayne was lying on the floor not moving. There was blood all over him. Streaming from his nose and mouth.

****

That night Wayne's mother was in the hospital waiting room. She was there to hear the results of her son's operation.

A doctor and nurse came into the waiting room. The doctor stood in front of Wayne's mother.

'I'm afraid it's not good news,' he said. 'Wayne's off the danger list but there's a lot of brain damage.'

Wayne's mother put her hand to her mouth, shocked.

The doctor waited before adding, 'I'm afraid the brain damage is so bad that he may not be able to walk. And we don't know yet, but he may not even be able to talk.'

'That bloody teacher,' sobbed Wayne's mother, 'I'll see he's locked up for life. Hitting my poor Wayne like that for no good reason. It's not right. It's just not right. Wayne's always been a good boy. He's never been in any trouble. Everyone loves him.'

****

Six months later Wayne's friend Jack was standing in the witness box. Swaggering and smirking.

A lot of his friends were watching from the public gallery. To Jack this was a right laugh. He was a bit of a star. Jack kept looking at his friends. Giving them the thumbs up. He was enjoying himself.

One of the barristers said to Jack, 'You know you have to speak the truth?'

Jack smiled and said, 'Yeah man. Be cool!'

Jack turned and pointed both his hands at the judge. With his thumbs up and trying to sound like a rap star he drawled, 'Be cool brother. Would I lie to you lot?'

In a loud voice the judge said, 'Young man, this is not the school playground. If you keep acting the fool I will have you arrested. I can put you in prison if you do not do exactly as I say. What is more, it will not be next week, or next month. You will be in prison within the next hour.'

Jack stopped smiling.

'Now, young man,' said the judge firmly, 'do you understand me?'

Jack stood up straight and nodded.

'Very well,' said the judge, 'that's better, now let's start again.'

The judge then nodded at the barrister.

Looking at Jack, the barrister said again, 'Now, you know you have to speak the truth?'

This time Jack just said, 'Yes.' It was almost a whisper.

'Speak up young man,' said the judge firmly. 'Everybody needs to hear what you say.'

'Yes,' said Jack, this time in a louder voice.

'Now take your time,' said the barrister. 'Don't rush it. Tell us exactly what happened before Mr Martin attacked Wayne.'

'Well,' said Jack, 'me and Wayne were in the bogs.'

The barrister held up his hand. 'Let's just try and use words that everybody in the court will understand. What is a bog?'

'Sorry,' said Jack, 'the bog's the place in school where we go for a piss. Me and Wayne were in there. We were 'avin' a fag just before our history lesson.'

The barrister shook his head but said nothing. Jack carried on.

'Wayne asked me what the next lesson was.

An' I said history. Then Wayne said, "It's not bloody old Fartin again is it?" And I just laughed.'

The barrister looked at Jack, 'What was that?' he snapped.

Now Jack looked worried. This was not going anything like the way he wanted it to.

'That's what me and Wayne used to call Mr Martin. We called him "old Fartin". We was always taking the piss out of him.'

'After we'd finished our fags I said to Wayne that we could jazz things up a bit. Next lesson when we was taking the piss out of old Fartin, I'd film it. We were going to stick

it up on YouTube. Just for a bit of a laugh,'
he added, almost in a whisper.

The judge said loudly, 'Young man. You need
to speak up. I don't want to have to ask
again.'

Jack was beginning to look sorry for himself.
He spoke in a louder voice.

'It was then that Wayne said, "Yeah. Nice one.
Let's go jazz it up with old Fartin." Or
something like that. When we got to the
classroom Mr Martin had already started
the lesson.' said Jack.

'Straight away Mr Martin began shouting at
us. He said something like, "Where've you

two been? You're late. Find yourself a seat and sit down." I could tell he was fed up. Wayne and me went and sat at two desks in the front of the class.'

Jack stopped talking for a moment. A woman at the back of the court cleared her throat. The sound echoed around the quiet courtroom.

'Then,' Jack went on, 'Wayne said something like, "Take it easy man. We were just having a couple of spliffs in the bogs. No need for you to go nuts." I started laughing. As we sat down Wayne said, "Feel free to carry on Mr Fartin." The whole class was laughing.'

The barrister said, 'You mean Wayne called

him "Mr Fartin"? To his face? In front of the class?'

'Yes,' said Jack shrugging his shoulders.

'Then what happened?' asked the barrister.

'Well Mr Martin was going on an' on about this bloke Hitler. Then Wayne said some stuff about Hitler and Mr Martin went nuts. He just lost it.'

'And you filmed all this?' asked the barrister. 'That's the film we've all seen? This was all part of a plan cooked up by you and Wayne. You both planned it.'

★★★★

Four days later the trial was nearly finished. Mr Martin was sitting in the dock. He looked like a broken man. His head was bowed, as if he was afraid of the judge.

Looking at Mr Martin the judge said, 'You need to stand up Mr Martin.'

Mr Martin slowly got to his feet. His arms hung limply at his sides.

'The jury has found you guilty of attempted murder,' said the judge. 'You should not have attacked the boy in the way you did.'

The judge hesitated and waited for Mr Martin to look at him.

'What you did was very wrong,' he went on.

The judge glanced down at his notes and then back at Mr Martin before saying, 'This kind of crime demands a long time in prison. We have been told that Wayne will never be able to walk again. It is also likely he will be unable to talk. What you did was truly, truly awful.'

The courtroom fell deathly silent for a moment.

'So, Mr Martin,' said the judge, 'I sentence you to ten years in prison.'

Some people in the gallery clapped.

Wayne's mother shouted, 'That's right. Send him down. I hope the bugger rots.'

The judge banged his gavel on the table. 'Silence!' he boomed.

When things had gone quiet, the judge went on. 'However, there are a few more things I wish to say.'

He looked at Mr Martin.

'What these boys planned and did was wicked. They tried to make you look helpless and foolish. What is more, we have heard that these two boys had done this to you before.'

The judge turned his head to look at Jack who was sitting at the front of the court.

'We have also heard,' he went on, 'that these two boys have done this to other school teachers, on many occasions.'

The judge looked back at Mr Martin.

'We have heard from other teachers that you have never done anything like this before. You have been an excellent teacher for many years. Always doing the best for your pupils.'

The judge looked out at all the people in the court.

'We have also heard from a number of your

former pupils. Some are sitting in the court today. They were all full of praise for you.'

The judge shook his head, 'It is very sad to see that you have ended up here.'

A murmur rippled around the court and some people nodded their heads.

'However, both of these boys must take a share in the blame for what happened. I am sorry that Wayne was hurt so badly. But it is important to note that the reason we are all here today is largely due to the deliberate actions of these two boys.'

Again there was another murmur.

'What you did was wrong Mr Martin,' said the judge. 'But you were not entirely to blame. You were provoked. Getting sacked from a job you love is a punishment in itself.'

Mr Martin looked up at this remark. He held his breath for just a second before the judge began to talk again.

'Therefore, Mr Martin, this will be a suspended sentence.'

The judge added, 'You are free to go.'

Wayne's mother jumped to her feet screaming, 'You can't do that! It's not fair. That bugger should go to jail. Look at what he did to my Wayne.'

The judge banged on his desk and shouted, 'Silence.'

When the court was quiet the judge said, 'I'd like Jack to be brought back to the witness box. I have something more to say to him.'

Jack was led back to the box. This time looking very worried. The judge turned to him.

'You were an important part of the planning of this event. Wayne was the one who threw insults at Mr Martin. But you were a willing helper and even filmed it.'

The judge shook his head and went on, 'Clearly, you were a key part of the plan.

Because of this plan Mr Martin, a good teacher, has lost his job. His wife and children have been badly affected.'

Jack could hardly bring himself to look the judge in the eye now.

'We have also heard that Mr Martin has, in the past, helped a number of pupils at your school. Yet now, as a direct result of your actions, future pupils have been robbed of his support.'

The judge looked directly at Jack and said firmly, 'Mr Martin is now unemployed. What's more, he's unlikely to get another teaching job.'

The judge looked down at his notes again before saying, 'It is true that perhaps Wayne has suffered the most. But, he was part of the plan. A plan that you both cooked up.'

A few of Jack's friends who were sat in the court began looking at each other.

'Because of what you did, Wayne's mother will suffer by having to look after him. Probably for the rest of her life. '

'Therefore, it is my belief that you are partly to blame. The police may wish to consider a charge of affray.' The judge quickly banged his gavel on the table and said, 'Case closed.'

****

Jack gave a sigh of relief. He was free to go. He stepped down from the witness box and walked out of the court with his parents.

On the steps outside all his friends gathered round him. They were clapping him on the back saying what a great guy he was.

Jack was beginning to feel good again. He could see that his friends thought he'd been cool. A grin spread over his face as he gave one of his mates a high-five. They all laughed.

A big crowd of Jack's friends were still shaking his hand and slapping his back when two police officers walked up to Jack. His face fell.

One of the policemen said, 'I'm arresting you on suspicion of affray.'

He then cuffed Jack, and took him away.

In the police station Jack was formally charged.

★★★★

The punishment for causing an affray can be a long prison sentence.

Jack was not granted bail. He was sent to prison where he has been waiting three months for a trial date.

★★★★